TICKER KHAN

Bamber Gascoigne

ILLUSTRATIONS BY PAULINE MARTIN

SIMON AND SCHUSTER
NEW YORK

Designed by Eve Metz
Manufactured in the United States of America

1 2 3 4 5 6 7 8 9 10

Library of Congress Cataloging in Publication Data

Gascoigne, Bamber.
Ticker Khan.
I. Title.
PZ4.G2465Ti3   [PR6057.A724]   823'.9'14   74-26902
ISBN 0-671-21963-4

I imagine that even in the very beginnings of time there were pheasants who wondered about the meaning of existence and Man's inscrutable ways. It may be that then, as now, the average bone-headed young cock was content to scratch and preen through a humdrum round of pleasures with never a thought for the morrow. But surely no bird with even a modicum of real intelligence can have avoided becoming deeply disturbed, at some time in his brief span on earth, by the central and eternal problem of life—that paradox which our philosophers have summed up under two irreconcilable headings, the Summer Truth and the Winter Truth.

THE SUMMER TRUTH. Man rules the Estate in which we live, and we are His chosen creatures. He protects us from fox, from weasel and from hoody crow. He rears us from egg to chick to full-fledged adolescent. He feeds us with His own hand.

There is no other bird in His woods of which this is true. And as if to justify His preference, we grow into the most beautiful of His creatures.

THE WINTER TRUTH. Man rules the Estate in which we live, and we are His victims. His love for us withers with the leaves. One day he drives us from those very copses where He has scattered our morning grain. He shoots us in our hundreds. He has changed, as if overnight, from Creator to Destroyer.

How to explain such a change?

This is the question with which each of our four major religions has grappled. Each has provided its own answer. Each can now be shown to be inadequate.

⌘

No pheasant has pondered these difficult matters more deeply than Ticker Khan, and it is entirely fitting that to him the Truth was finally revealed. This little book of mine is an account of that Revelation.

If you ask any young pheasant which among us has survived the greatest number of Ordeals, he will be certain to answer Ticker Khan, and I would hasten to add that this upright old bird, an example to us all, has richly deserved his reputation—even though, strictly speaking, it may be based on a very minor and unimportant error of fact. I have reason to believe that I myself may be a year older than Ticker Khan, but as I have little to be proud of in my method of survival I have always avoided making much of my age. With what we now know about proper conduct, my behavior at each Ordeal seems even more shameful. But the time for confession will be later.

When I say Ordeal I refer, of course, only to Great Ordeals, when we are driven from the woods and copses toward the waiting line of Men with guns. We have on our Estate three Great Ordeals every year, in the autumn and early winter, and in those we are each of us, whether we like it or not, unavoidably involved. Lesser ordeals, in which a few Men walk with dogs, are far more numerous. But any bird who gets entangled in one of these rather arbitrary affairs has only himself to blame.

Ticker Khan has told us how, on a bitterly cold day last winter, he felt an overwhelming desire to learn the Truth. It was the sort of day when the preachers of our four old religions were out, knowing they could be sure of an audience. Two of the Ordeals had passed, and everyone sensed that the third must soon be upon us. Tensions such as this will incline almost any bird toward metaphysical speculation—even, no doubt, some of those witless young hens who in the balmy days of this present spring and summer could hardly be persuaded to lend an ear to the actual Truth after it had been discovered. Moreover, the frost had got into the ground deeper than the length of a beak. If there were grubs down there, that was where they were staying. So the preachers could rely on full congregations at the various places where the Keeper scatters our corn.

We seem less inclined to scramble for food in our old age, and Ticker tells us that throughout that day not a single grain passed his gullet, even though he spent all his time at the feeding places. It was as though appetite had shifted from his crop to his brain. He had a sudden hunger for any new word that the rival sects might offer him.

He began where he felt most at home, among the Peacock Revivalists, for this was the sect into which he had been born. He found them in their usual place, where the bridge of tree trunks crosses the stream at the far end of the beech wood. This was where he had always eaten his winter grain, and even in his present mood he was happy to greet the grandchildren of several of his oldest friends. They were all natural-born pheasants here, of course.

Dribel Khan was droning on as usual, telling the story of the Great Peacock—as if everybody had not heard it a hundred times before, Ticker said to himself in his irritation that morning, though he now points out that he was unjust in rejecting the repetition as such. Ritual, which to deserve the name must consist almost entirely of repetition, is an important part of every religion. The only crux is the truth of what is being repeated. And, beautiful though the story was that the famous Cocker Khan had brought back from his travels so many years ago, Ticker had never felt that it could carry much weight as a guide to modern life. He was prepared to admit that a creature as grand and magnificent as the Peacock might actually exist. Indeed there was a pleasing lesson in humility in the very idea of its existence. Man, the Superior Being, bears no physical resemblance to ourselves at all, and any comparison in the matter of appearance between Him and us is therefore meaningless to the point of irrelevance. All that we can say about ourselves is that the healthy cock pheasant, in his prime, is the most spectacular *bird* that has ever been seen by any living creature. But we have no pattern by which to judge how near to perfection we may be. How apt, then, to postulate an even more magnificent bird beside which we may become aware of our own infirmities. We may almost say, in philosophical terms, that the existence of such a bird is a necessary existence. And then, in the mists of unrecorded time, infinite generations ago, the fabled Cocker Khan flew here from far away with his staggering piece of information. He had met such a creature, and it was called a Peacock. Philosophy, myth, religion and epic all seemed to have come together in a perfectly satisfying image, and the details of the story were in keeping with the wonder of it.

Cocker Khan, exhausted and far from home, had landed to rest his wings among some beautiful flowers (almost as bright as ourselves, so the story went), which stood in a broad clump along the edge of a wide expanse of grass. Looking out, he saw that on the other side of the grass there stood a Great House of some faraway Estate, presumably containing a Man. He was about to run for cover when he observed, to his utter amazement, the most remarkable pheasant he had ever set eyes upon. Larger than us, brighter than us, even more beautiful than us, it was actually sitting on the window-sill of the House and looking in. Mesmerized by such courage, Cocker Khan seems to have lost his own fear. He walked slowly across the grass toward the House. The great bird eyed him, saying nothing. Cocker Khan stopped where the grass turned to flagstones, feeling that it might be improper for him to advance closer. The conversation that followed has clearly been refined by time and constant retelling, as is the way with myth, but I record it here as it has always within living memory been narrated and as Ticker no doubt heard it once again that morning last winter.

"Is there a Man in that House?" asked Cocker Khan.

"Yes," replied the imperturbable bird.

"Then why do you look in?"

"There is also a Peacock, like myself, in there."

"Does the Man shoot at you?"

"Why on earth should He?"

"I don't know."

"Then why do you ask?"

At this point, the story goes, the Peacock did the most extraordinary thing—some say to give irrefutable proof of his greater beauty, others just as a way of signaling that the interview was over, the impertinence already more than sufficient. He somehow raised his tail, already impressive by its length, into a huge and dazzling fan behind him. Moreover, there were eyes in this tail, believed later by the Peacock Revivalists to be the eyes with which he could perceive truths obscured from us.

And then, in the most alarming manner, he rattled this tail at Cocker Khan, who reported that the whole thing seemed to shimmer and that there was a sound like the wind rustling stalks of ripe corn. I myself believe, if there is any truth at all in the story, that the opening of the tail was to demonstrate superior beauty and that the rustling of it, which sounds rather threatening, was the sign to Cocker Khan that it was time to go. Certainly he took the hint, and with three quick strides over the grass he was up and away.

There was a time when nearly all our ancestors were of Cocker Khan's faith, believing that Man's wish was for each one of His natural-born pheasants to grow into the more perfect form of a Peacock, and that once this was achieved He would cease to shoot us and would allow us, like the First Peacock, into His House.

Ticker Khan's problem, and one that I wholeheartedly shared, was to see how this charming idea could be turned into sensible actions which might help a pheasant on the day of an Ordeal. Nice though it would no doubt be to become a Peacock, what were we to do to achieve that end? Certainly the practical effect on some of the younger Peacock Revivalists was far from encouraging. There were a few vain creatures, for example, who convinced themselves that the secret lay in the spreading of the tail. A pheasant who could do this, they argued, would actually by definition *be* a Peacock, and they engaged in long and futile sessions to develop the muscles of their rear. The most that anyone achieved was a ludicrous cocking of the entire stern straight up into the air, somewhat reminiscent of a robin.

At the other extreme, the more thoughtful among the Peacock Revivalists evolved what was almost a form of nihilism by concentrating on the last two lines of the text: *I don't know. Then why do you ask?* They pointed out that this is a very marked reversal of the logical sequence, which would be either *I don't know. Then ask.* or *I know. Then why do you ask?* They believed, therefore, that the whole burden of the Peacock's message was the necessity of blind acceptance. We should not inquire, they argued, about that which is, and was no doubt meant to remain, obscure. In practical terms this led a handful of misguided pheasants to fly limply toward the guns on the day of an Ordeal, on the ground that what must be must be, with someone else presumably in possession of the reason why. Fortunately this flabby attitude never caught on with more than a very few birds, and those no doubt ones that we could well do without. Otherwise the Peacock Revivalists might have a great deal to answer for.

The majority of the sect, including Ticker himself, interpreted the myth to mean that pheasants must imitate the courage and magnificence of the Peacock if they are ever to acquire his appearance, and indeed his identity. It is for this reason that Ticker Khan has in the past always flown straight over the line of guns, high and fast, in company with other like-minded aristocrats. (Here is perhaps the moment to say something about the notorious exclusivity of Peacock Revivalism, which has often given offense, for it was a faith closed to any but natural-born birds. The Revivalists argued, with some logic, that if the whole purpose of a pheasant's span on earth is to rise to the status of a Peacock, then any bird of such humble background as a foster-fowl stands less than a reasonable chance. The restriction on membership, they would explain, was to avoid disappointment as much as anything else.)

Pecking absentmindedly at a couple of young cocks who had come too close, Ticker Khan strolled away along the edge of the stream in the direction that would bring him to the new plantation of larch. More than ever he felt this morning a deep sense of disillusion with the Peacock Revivalists, yet intertwined with this there was also a feeling of loss. These were, after all, his own people, fighting cocks like himself. How often had he led parties of those young birds, now many of them themselves quite long in beak and spur, in boundary skirmishes against pheasants of the neighboring estate! And how he wished this very morning that he could share their simple and romantic belief in the Great Peacock. It fitted so well with the other glorious traditions of pheasantry which had meant so much to him—the legend, for example, that our ancestors came from some distant land far more magnificent in every respect than this humdrum home of thrushes and blackbirds. I say legend, yet I personally believe this to be history, and I think Ticker Khan would agree. What other birds in the whole world have Khan after their names? There must be something in that. It all seemed to fit, if one were in the right mood, in a most satisfactory manner. Yet as Ticker Khan has pointed out, even if the Great Peacock did exist, he never actually said that he was himself a better kind of pheasant. This was an entirely subjective assumption on the part of his followers, deriving from the fact that he seems to have been more like a pheasant than anything else we know. He himself never even hinted as much. In fact, to be absolutely frank— in an area where frankness used to be none too common—Ticker Khan has more than once observed to me that if we are to go by the received text alone, the Great Peacock does not even seem to have liked Cocker Khan, let alone recognized in him some sort of cousin. His reception, in Ticker Khan's opinion and my own, fell short even of the most elementary courtesy.

In the larch wood Ticker Khan came to the place where the Morsels meet. The preacher that day was Dreer Khan, without exception the most boring old bird that in my many months of life I have ever met. I feel free to speak of him with disrespect, because he is dead (he was one of the many that fell in the latest Ordeal).

The vision on which the Morsels based their faith was considerably more recent than Cocker Khan's meeting with the Peacock. I personally believe that it occurred as a direct result of Peacock Revivalism and that the Morsels should therefore be regarded as the main offshoot of the earlier and perhaps once universal faith, but Dreer Khan always hotly disputed this interpretation. Be that as it may, the simple historical fact is that in comparatively recent times a young cock by the name of Flapper Khan flew with very great courage in the middle of the day to alight on one of the ground-floor windowsills of the Great House on our own Estate. Many a time have I argued to Dreer Khan that he must have done so in imitation of the Peacock, hoping to see what he saw inside, namely the other Peacock. But Dreer Khan used to insist that he did so only because he did so, adding that one could say no more.

Everyone agrees that Flapper did not see a Peacock. But he did see something equally thought-provoking—a corpse. It was lying, in a state of

rigor mortis but surprisingly neatly arranged, on a brown shiny surface somewhat to the right of the window. One of the oddest things about it, distinguishing it utterly from any other corpse which you might find in the woods, was that the parts which are normally left to the last had in this case been eaten first—in other words the head, claws and feathers were all missing, but the flesh itself seemed remarkably intact.

Those who did not share the faith of the Morsels always argued that with the body in this unheard-of condition it was impossible for Flapper Khan to say with any certainty that this was a corpse, and not just a carcass of some other sort of creature. But the Morsels, exercising the prerogative of faith, were convinced that it was a pheasant, and there are certain facts which would seem to support their case.

One is that a considerable number of corpses are indeed carried every winter into the Great House. The invariable sequence of events is as follows. The fallen in each Ordeal are suspended in rows in a small hut behind the Great House, the windows of which are covered in a fine mesh. The Morsels, over the generations, have kept this hut under close observation and they have established beyond any possible doubt that on a certain day the comrades hanging along the two sides of the hut are all packed into large hampers and taken away down the drive, to none knows where. But those hanging on the end wall remain there until they are carried, in two and threes, into the Great House. And since there appears to be nothing that a corpse is any good for except to be eaten, the Morsels used to argue with some plausibility that the only possible reason why Man took them into the House was to eat them—or, more precisely, to eat their heads, claws and feathers, the three visible components of a pheasant's beauty, in some ultimate ceremony of Union. The chosen few, set apart on the end wall for Man to take unto Himself, were known as the True or Blessed Morsels.

It was not known how these fortunate few were selected, but two well-documented facts formed the basis of the Morsels' belief on the subject. One is that Man seems most pleased at the death of a pheasant when that pheasant has been flying very high and fast; then Men raise Their hats to each other, and have even been known to throw them in the air, a gesture which is believed to imply the highest approval. The other is that the pheasants carried into the Great House are almost without exception young birds. Young birds fly higher and faster than their elders, and it has therefore been argued that Man reserves His approval for those who die at a great height.

Thus the aristocratic Peacock Revivalists and the egalitarian Morsels found common cause. Both, on the day of a Great Ordeal, would exert themselves to fly as high and as fast as possible. It was their motives that were diametrically opposed. The young Ticker Khan and his friends hoped so to impress Man that He would spare them and hasten their change into Peacocks. The Morsels hoped so to impress Man that He would select them for His Table.

I suppose that the Morsels, among all our old sects, were the best loved. Not only for their courage, their calmness in the face of death. No, it was as much as anything else for their egalitarianism. Background counted for nothing among the Morsels. Seeing that birds of every class, whether natural-born or foster-fowl, could reach the end wall, and believing that they got there by their own efforts alone, a sincere Morsel cared nothing for the conventional divisions within society. Naturally I myself welcomed this, but I mention it not with any sense of grievance or chip on my shoulder. When I say that I too am a foster-fowl, I hope that I am stating a fact, not making a statement. I am the first to recognize that coming from an egg the origins of which are unknown, and being reared by a tame chicken in a coop, are precisely the type of disabilities which will lead to class distinctions in any community. And when lines have to be drawn, as in the coming autumn parade, class is certainly as good a criterion as any other. I am only saying that among the many old creeds which none of us now believe in, it is not surprising that the Morsels appealed most widely. It was certainly a church in which you could meet a very nice type of bird.

❦

That same day, still fasting, Ticker dallied for a while among the Seekers of the Sun, up by the Douglas fir at the top of the hill. The Seekers had the most elaborate ritual of any of our sects, but there was a marked lack of intellectual rigor in their thesis. They observed that Man is gentle in the summer, when the Sun lingers many hours, and that He becomes cruel when the days are short, and they argued from this that His mood must be influenced by the Sun. Indeed they saw the Sun itself as a sort of Man, a Man set above Men in the heavens. This was why they indulged in their performances at the top of the Douglas fir, begging the Sun at dusk not to desert them, and at dawn welcoming it back. It was a most unsuitable tree for a pheasant, consisting of a mass of very sharp and dusty twigs (a Seeker friend once persuaded me

to try one of the lower branches—never again). I believe they just perched up there and prayed and bobbed about according to certain long-established patterns. I remember once there was an extraordinarily hot and beautiful summer, and the Seekers claimed it was thanks to their efforts and that Man would now be appeased. It was immediately followed by one of the most brutal Ordeals that have ever been known. One or two of the more intellectual Seekers did move to another sect, but most of them just sat where they were and vowed to pray even harder.

᭜

Ticker also visited briefly the Chicks of the Keeper, down in the copse by the bottom meadow with its reassuring clumps of bracken and gorse. The Chicks used to gather there because it is near the Keeper's cottage. Their faith was based on a type of dualism. They believed that the Keeper, who feeds us, represents all that is good in Man—and the Man in the House, Who shoots us, all that is evil (or "the man in the house," as they would insist on writing Him, which caused considerable offense). They liked to point out that the Keeper also has a house, albeit a very small one. Two years ago the Keeper's cottage did suddenly grow larger

at the back, and not much later a considerable section to one side of the Great House was taken down. These events caused untold excitement among the Chicks. They held that as the Keeper's powers for goodness grew, so would his house, while that of the Man would continue to shrink, until one distant day the Keeper would have a huge house and the Man a tiny one, by which time, they said, the Keeper would in effect have become the Man and a new Reign of Goodness would have begun.

There were obvious flaws in this argument. To begin with, the division between Good and Evil was overly simple. The Keeper has been known to shoot us; the Man in the Great House has been known to feed us; and on the day of an Ordeal it is the Keeper who drives us out of the copse toward the Man. Moreover it would be just as reasonable to argue that the Keeper will become more evil as his house grows larger, and that once he is living in a Great House things will be just as they are now. If this were true, no change would be possible and there would be no point in religion.

❦

"There would be no point in religion." This is perhaps the moment to admit how many of us—above all the intellectuals, and myself, I freely confess, among them—have sunk in the past to such depths of despair that we have doubted whether any religion can provide the answer to the Pheasant's Predicament. In the darker moods of youth I was able to believe, at one and the same moment, all religions and none. I have in my day argued coherently that our life here on this Estate is intrinsically pointless, a brief interlude of corn, courtship and preening (or greed, lust and vanity) between eggshell and worms. And yet at the very same time I have found it perfectly possible to imagine that all the wilder fantasies of the old religions were true—that somewhere there really are Peacocks (themselves, in that case, subject to greed, lust and vanity), that Man does eat the pheasants He loves, that sunshine will improve His temper, and that the Keeper is perhaps the better of the two Men. In my blackest hours I even believed that I had solved the paradox by the simple expedient of denying that any paradox exists. I argued then that the central contradiction of our lives (that Man should rear us in the spring and shoot us in the autumn) is only an apparent contradiction, which vanishes instantly if one postulates a totally cynical Man who rears us precisely because He later intends to shoot us. For a few terrible days, at the age of about one and a half, I chose to see Him that way.

How merciful then are the ways of Man and of His prophet Ticker Khan that I, miserable sinner, blinded with intellectual pride, a doubter and in my time even a satirist, should now be entrusted to bring you, my elegant and beloved reader, the simple and joyous truth as revealed to Ticker Khan and expressed, for those who are not faint of heart, in those glorious words that can now be heard any one of these summer mornings echoing round our woodlands.

THERE SHALL BE NO MORE DEATH!

Ticker Khan had heard not a single phrase from any preacher to satisfy his hunger for the Truth, as he walked about the feeding places on that blessed morn. Later, when the day's grain was finished and the assemblies had dispersed, he moved silently among the small groups of pheasants which can always be found, in the period before an Ordeal, arguing about the best chances for safety when the moment arrives.

He himself, on such occasions, had discussed with his friends only how to achieve maximum height and speed before streaming straight over the very center of the line of guns. It is a hard thing for a pheasant to fly like this. We are heavy birds, with strong legs, and whenever it is at all convenient we prefer to walk rather than fly. That is why you could never see Ticker and his friends practicing the great flights which they achieved on the day of an Ordeal. To get that ultimate touch of speed is a matter of highly technical detail, such as the most streamlined position for beak, head and neck, or how to get the wind under one's tail and trap it there. But the business of clattering up almost vertically from the undergrowth, fighting through leaves and branches that seem to splinter about one's face, and throwing the body forward and out into the open, all this (I am told) is made possible only by that final charge of excitement in the bowels on the actual day. It cannot be rehearsed.

So Ticker was profoundly shocked when he walked that afternoon among the many groups and heard them discussing something very different—how to survive at any price. Some were giving tips to each other (or even more likely keeping tips from each other) as to the various places where a bird could sneak out of a copse or spinney between the narrowing lines of beaters and guns without being troubled by either. Some were arguing that the only safe way was to get down to the stream and to run along as near as possible to the edge of the water. Some were even advocating that most terrifying of all techniques, in which one chooses a thick clump of gorse down in the low meadow and sits it out, come what may. I tried this once, when I was a very young bird. Never again. Two dogs caught scent of me, not just one. I might have shifted about the bush a bit if there had been only one. But there they were on each side, poking those unbelievable beaks they have (wet *and* soft) straight in among the prickles. I just squatted, convinced that my end had come. Five inches from my right eyeball were those flaring black nostrils. Even closer to my left eye, on the other side of the bush, a great flat pink tongue giving off *steam*. Then, Man be praised for His mercy, they were called off.

You will no doubt expect that I, an intellectual, was one of those found by Ticker Khan that day feverishly discussing means of escape. But I was not. I regret to say that after my experience in the gorse bush I devised my own method of escape, which I shared with no one. It is something that I am very far from proud of. But this is a time for truthfulness, and I might as well admit it here as elsewhere. I have long ago told Ticker Khan the full story, and he was gracious enough to overlook it—perhaps because one small aspect of my method was, indirectly, of some use to himself and to the Cause.

As an intellectual, I had succeeded in analyzing a phenomenon which had often been observed but never explained. At certain intervals during the winter the Keeper places out rows of sticks, standing upright in the ground, each with a cleft in the top in which some sort of white label is fixed. This had always been regarded as a random event, as natural as the clouds passing by or the wind blowing up and dying down. My one insight, which no doubt would have brought me fame if I had not selfishly kept it to myself, was to observe that a Great Ordeal invariably took place the very day after the sticks had been placed out. I had no idea if there was any causal connection, as I had never stayed to observe what use might be made of those sticks, but I had established beyond any doubt at all that there was a sequential link.

I realize, elegant reader, how shocked you will be to hear that I kept from our own kind a scientific discovery which would undoubtedly, in the short term, have saved many lives. I can plead only abject fear and self-interest. I calculated that if we all vanished on the day of an Ordeal, the Keeper would know that the signal of the cleft sticks had been interpreted and he might never put them out again. At each subsequent Ordeal I would then be no better off than any other bird.

Instead, during the night which followed the appearance of the sticks, I used to make my way by

devious routes, arousing no one's suspicions, to the very edge of the Estate, where I waited till first light. Then I hurried across a mysterious broad expanse of congealed grit—a terrifying place where objects hurtle about at more than twice the speed of flight, with Men inside—and on the other side I found myself among strange fields. I have rarely had to walk far to find one with turnips or kale in it. And there, grubbing around between the furrows, I used to spend an ignominious but quiet day among the partridges. You will not need me to describe the sense of degradation, even for an intellectual. But survival has its attractions, too. And I am now five years old.

None of this, my personal shame, did Ticker Khan know till later. Even so, he has told me that he was profoundly saddened by all the more humdrum discussion of hiding and escape that he heard as he went his rounds that day. Being himself an aristocrat and an athlete, with good looks to match, he had lived his life on the basis that magnificence was the natural birthright of the pheasant. And now, on a bitterly cold winter's day, with nothing in his crop, he came suddenly into contact with all the petty evasions which the rest of us know to be the natural order of things among the middle classes.

Dusk found him in a state of extreme distress, and it must have been this, combined with the disorientation brought on by fasting, which led him to take his most unusual step. Night fell. The rest of us had long since flown up into the trees to roost. Those familiar but eerie sounds swelled up around him, of owl and badger and bat, and still he was pacing on the carpet of beech leaves below. A great moon rose. The snow-covered field outside the wood glowed with light, so that anyone still awake could have seen the branches of the trees silhouetted sharply against the ground. And then Ticker Khan did something which probably no pheasant has ever done before. He walked out into an open field at night.

Very slowly, with his usual great dignity and possibly even in a state of trance, he stepped from the shelter of the beech trees into the vast expanse of white. There were about two inches of snow and a new sprinkling had fallen a little earlier, so it spread like an unsullied cloth before him. He must have stepped high, placing each foot straight down into the snow and then lifting it just as vertically out again, because those who observed his tracks the next day say that each mark was perfectly clear, three unblurred fingers and a toe behind, like a sign. There was no trace of that feathery elongation of the central line which we usually make when we walk in deep snow, through dragging our claw between steps. Maybe the whole walk took him several hours. We shall never know. He has no recollection of the passage of time. And no one was watching.

He was making his way, again perhaps subconsciously, to the corner of the field where the Keeper stores the pens and coops from one breeding season to the next. The big pens of timber and wire lay on their sides, with snow encrusting the top edge and other little fluffs of it trapped among the mesh like blobs of moonlight. In a row behind them were the hutches, also white-topped on their tiny sloping roofs. The slatted grilles were in place, which when the hutch was joined to a pen would enable all of us, as youngsters, to run freely to and fro, inside or outside at will, while our pathetic foster-mother, a dusty old farmyard chicken, was trapped within. Beside the hutches were the metal containers in which the drinking water always stays miraculously at the same height, on dry day or wet, and the new feeding trays in which, it is generally admitted, today's young pheasants have been getting better rations than ever.

These tender structures of wood and wire, lying before Ticker Khan so ghostly in the moonlight, are veritable treasure houses of memory. They evoke images of home, warmth, security, a cozy breast and the helping hand. I speak of course mainly for us foster-fowls, but for natural-born birds too, like Ticker Khan, it is impossible to feel indifferent toward this mighty nursery. An aristocrat may argue, probably with justification, that a hutch can bear no comparison to a nest in the bracken which has been individually created by loving parents. But the fact remains, and no bird will deny it, that but for the Keeper's pens our race would long since have died out. On our Estate alone some fifteen hundred little ones are bred each year to a healthy adolescence, before coming to join the rest of us in the woods.

Thus, in this nostalgic and moonlit scene, was Ticker Khan confronted by a most poignant image of the inscrutability of Man. The night was cold and steely bright, and full of the dread which always comes just before an Ordeal. It had the feel of death, Man's harshest offering. And yet here also, looking so mysteriously beautiful in this light, were the instruments of His other gift to us, our birth.

It is hardly surprising that this was to be the occasion of the Revelation which was vouchsafed

to Ticker Khan. No doubt the moment of insight lasted no longer than it takes to draw the inner lid across an eye, but Ticker Khan has recently set down for us the full sequence of thoughts which then flashed through his mind.

He remembers his eye falling on one of the new feeding trays, and the thought—in itself a perfectly familiar one—that Man is now providing the young pheasants with better food than ever before. There followed naturally the question, Why is He providing us with better food? So as to create better pheasants. But why does He want to create better pheasants? Certainly not in order to kill them. Presumably so that there shall actually *be* better pheasants; so that pheasants shall become truly *better*. And yet he does kill us. Why? Is it from disappointment? Is it because we fail to live up to the standards He has set for us? Is it because, in spite of the improved feeding, we have not *succeeded* in becoming better? And yet what are those standards of His to which we must more nearly conform? In what way, when it comes to the crunch, can a pheasant like myself actually do better?

☦

Ticker Khan says that here, and this was clearly the beginning of the Revelation itself, he had an

overwhelming impression of his long-lost friend
Pecker. Pecker almost seemed, he tells us, to be
present there with him in the snow.

Pecker Khan, of course, has since been made the
patron saint of our movement. As a young bird,
from nest to final plumage, he had been the constant companion of Ticker Khan's early days. The
two proud young cocks had fought together,
grubbed for insects together, raided the shocks of
corn together, taunted us foster-fowls together,
and tried out together those newly broken voices

which carry so far through the woods. They were, in the language of stories, inseparable. And when the day of an Ordeal came, naturally they always flew together.

Ticker Khan likes to say now that a measure of Pecker's stature was that never once did he, Ticker, manage to fly as high or as fast as his friend. On the day of Pecker's death in a Great Ordeal they had come high together over the beech wood, using a little swirl of wind which was bouncing off the hillside beyond. Ticker says he has never felt so exhilarated. The pair of them seemed untouchable. Pecker was a few yards ahead of him and several feet higher, with the feathers of his tail vibrating from the speed. Their sharp beaks cleaved the cold winter air which then rushed, clear as ice, past their eyes and round their necks and plump bodies, to join up again where the claws were tucked up under the tail. If Ticker kept his beak anything but tightly clenched, he seemed to be swallowing the entire wind, and there came from the tip of it a whistling sound which prevented his hearing what was going on below. The Men with Their guns looked tiny from this height, like pine needles stuck in the ground. At least four seemed to be firing at himself and Pecker, to no avail. When they were already almost safe, Pecker, daredevil that he was, banked sharply to the left to tantalize the remaining Men, still out of range at the end of the line. Ticker followed him. They were moving too fast to fly the curve. They braced their wings and glided

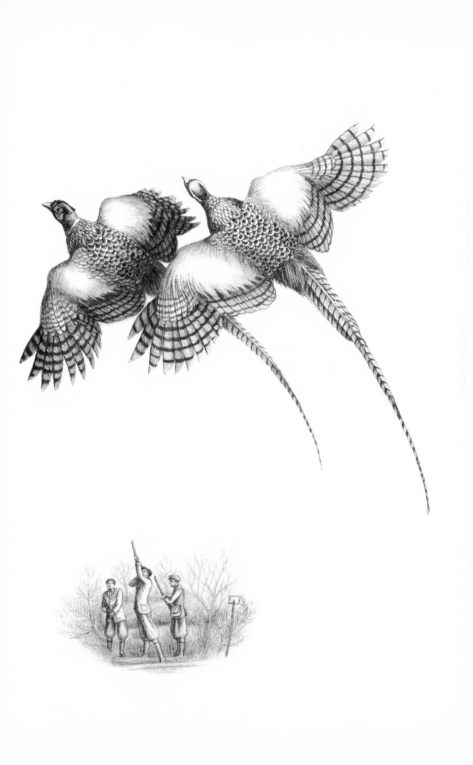

round, still unbelievably high and fast, as though they were a natural part of the wind. Ticker was positively enjoying himself now. And then, he says, Pecker suddenly seemed to pause and shudder in the air. There was a moment of shocked suspense, until his head fell forward, and still moving at great speed he performed a somersault of infinite grace. And another. And another. Each one of them like a movement which he had rehearsed. Ticker banked again, away from the line (and in doing so perhaps saved his life, since at this very moment some pellets tore away three of his wing feathers), and he looked back just in time to see Pecker crash onto the short-cropped grass of the field. He had seen the body bounce into the air again before the soft thump reached his ears, and then he was over the line of firs and safe.

Ticker Khan tells us that as he stood that moonlit night by the pens and coops, the image of Pecker that came to him so strongly was the moment when his head had fallen forward and he was beginning the first of his three spectacular somersaults. He had a macabre impression that as Pecker rolled forward, he looked up at him from under his crumpled wing. And he spoke.

"We believe, you and I, that Man shoots us only if we fail Him. But how have I failed Him, Ticker old chap, tell me that? No pheasant in history has ever flown as high or as fast or as magnificently as I; you yourself have said so many times. How could

I have done any better? What else could I have done?"

The moment passed. Pecker continued his roll forward, his next somersault, and his next, and as he hit the ground Ticker Khan seemed suddenly to awaken and to find himself standing in the snow by the rearing pens. Who can tell how long he had been there? All we know is that he had a quarter of an inch of snow on his head and along his back. And then, in this ghostly scene, Ticker seemed to hear his own voice—unmistakably his own, and yet outside himself. And he seemed to answer Pecker Khan.

"You could have walked, Pecker," he heard himself say. "YOU COULD HAVE WALKED."

※

Suddenly everything fell into place.

※

Of course. Pecker should have walked. No wonder Man was wrathful. If you take the trouble to create a living being, the very least you have a right to expect is that it will do its best to follow in your footsteps. Man provided pheasants with better and better food so that at last they might find the strength and courage to walk, moving just as Man Himself moves, slowly and with dignity, on the day of an Ordeal. That was the Test He had set. For to walk required even more courage than to fly. How could pheasants have been so blind over all these generations as not to see it? Instead the braver ones exerted themselves to fly higher and higher, and the rest sought out cowardly ways of sneaking to safety, both the very opposite of what Man intended. No wonder He was wrathful, after all that He had done for pheasants, when this sort of behavior went on year after year.

Pecker had been a martyr to a mistaken cause. Ticker Khan pledged himself there and then, in the middle of that field, to the memory of his old friend who had appeared to him in the vision. Let your heroic end, Pecker, he said, stand for all that can be achieved without enlightenment (and that is why he is now our patron saint), but let us who are enlightened ensure that there is never again such waste.

As Ticker Khan strode out of the field, formulating in his mind all that was to follow, he found a new pride and self-awareness in the very fact of walking. Suddenly he seemed to have discovered himself as a pheasant. The message fitted so precisely with what he had always instinctively felt.

He had been sustained all his life by a sense of the dignity of our race, and what movement is more dignified than walking? Everyone knows that pheasants prefer to walk rather than fly, but this has in the past been put down to idleness. Ticker Khan now saw that this much-criticized inclination was in reality an expression of our true dignity.

Does Man, when startled, take three quick strides and flap His thin but very agile wings to lift Himself laboriously into the air?

Then why should we?

Sparrows and robins, Ticker realized for the first time, and all those other little things that take to the air at the slightest provocation, are actually incapable of walking. They can only hop, a ludi-

crous movement if ever there was one. Partridges can sort of scurry about, and ducks with some difficulty flap their feet one in front of the other and waddle. But only pheasants and Man stride out, head held high, in a gait which perfectly expresses their shared dignity. The conclusion becomes even plainer if one puts it the other way round and asks, in the phrase that we have adopted as our slogan: "Who ever saw a Man fly?" From all that we know of Him, it is hardly likely that He is incapable of flying. He chooses not to. And the reason? A very simple one. It is not dignified. And long, and justly, has He punished us for not understanding this elementary fact.

Over the next few days Ticker Khan devoted himself, with untiring zeal, to spreading the word. Again and again he preached at each of the feeding-places. He told the manner of his Revelation. He expounded the irresistible logic of it. And he announced that on the day of the next Ordeal he himself, in sacred memory of Pecker Khan, would walk slowly and solemnly from the bottom of the beech wood straight toward *and through* the line of waiting guns.

It was a thankless task. Truth without proof makes a sorry pudding, as the saying goes. Ticker appealed for a hundred proud young cocks to accompany him, so as to prove to Man that it was not just one elderly eccentric, a pheasant calling in the wilderness, who had at last understood the message. Later he reduced his request to fifty, a dozen, even the odd two or three. Finally, and it shames me to write it, he was begging for a single hen pheasant to walk beside him. All he made himself, of course, was a laughingstock. I believe that for some it even enlivened those cheerless days to stand in small self-satisfied groups to either side of him as he spoke, twittering among themselves while his words of fire and passion were spent on the empty air.

Needless to say, the official preachers made him their butt. Whenever Ticker was in his vicinity, Dribel Khan would slowly and deliberately lift a foot to scratch behind his right ear while raising the other eye blankly to the heavens, an all too familiar gesture among young pheasants, as I know to my own cost, suggesting idiocy. And Dreer Khan, when Ticker was trying to convert the Morsels, could be relied on to announce in clarion tones that any bird who thought of walking toward the guns would undoubtedly (and for this he could take Dreer Khan's personal word) end up on one of the side walls. For he would certainly be shot, and no more inglorious death could be devised. To emphasize his words, Dreer Khan would pointedly move his neck forward and back as if walking. It is a movement of great elegance on a bird who is striding out, but it can be made to seem humorous if done while stationary. Dreer Khan's little charade was greeted by his audience with uncontrolled merriment. Such was the mood of those times. Yet I confess that even I, in my own quiet way, was seen on occasion to smile.

I am proud to tell, however, that I was able to render one small service. During the first day or two of his mission Ticker Khan had been haunted by the fear that the tap-tap-tapping of the trees (the first sign that an Ordeal is beginning) would be heard when he was preaching in some distant part of the Estate. For he had decided that his Walk must be carried out from the beech wood. In practical terms this was the only open space large enough for the whole line of men to see him as he approached, and from a mystical point of view I know that he was influenced by the thought that here Pecker had died, here Pecker had brought him the Revelation. It would be a disaster if he was unable to get back to the beech wood before the beaters began to drive it out.

Impressed even then, I suppose, by the old bird's evident sincerity, I decided to tell him my secret— though I made him promise, at that time, that he would keep it so. I told him that an Ordeal could not possibly occur until the split sticks were placed out, and that if he then returned to the beech wood he would have a full night and a dawn in which to replenish his strength. And so it turned out.

Although Ticker's message had gone unheeded, he had made himself very much the center of attention. It seemed that every bird on the Estate must have heard before the day of the Ordeal some version, however garbled, of what he planned to do. A great many pheasants, once the tap-tap-tapping began, abandoned, at considerable risk to themselves, the covers from which they had intended to fly and crowded into the beech wood, where they lined the thick belt of shrubs and long grass at its base. Thus it was that there were so many eyewitnesses of the Walk, and it is the reports of the few survivors, differing only in minor details, which have made it possible for me to compile here a definitive version of what happened—even though I myself was (for the last time) away among the partridges.

The beech wood was driven on that occasion early in the day. No pheasant had ever before deliberately watched the proceedings (each had been cowering somewhere on his own), but now the assembled company saw the Men walk into the field to take up their positions. And at last, incidentally, the meaning of the cleft sticks with the little white labels was found. Beside each of them a Man with a gun placed Himself. Then there was a long pause, which Ticker Khan says he found his most trying time. Nothing seemed to be happening. But finally, far back at the top of the wood, there was the sound of tapping. The beaters would not reach him for several minutes but Ticker had decided to move early, in case any young pheasant might be seized by panic and fly out before him. Complete stillness, undivided attention to himself, was essential.

So Ticker Khan parted the tuft of grass which

had been hiding him, and stepped forth. He stood
there in the open field, plain for all to see, with the
grass now not reaching even up to his spur. Nothing happened. It seemed that he had not even been
noticed, and he cursed himself for having failed to
convince those hundred young birds whom he had
imagined so clearly in his mind's eye lined up behind him. The Men could hardly have failed to observe a hundred and one cock pheasants standing
in a row at the edge of the field.

This, Ticker tells us, was his darkest moment.
The snow of eleven days ago had melted and the
field was wet. Mud oozed between his claws as he
trudged solemnly forward. No Man so much as

turned His head. No dog's nose lifted to scent the air. It suddenly felt, says Ticker, as though all his feathers had dropped off—as if he stood there, a naked and skinny old fowl, the laughingstock of his own kind in the woods behind, the certain and easy victim of a jealous Man ahead. Yes, reader, for a moment even Ticker Khan doubted. Even he wondered whether Pecker had really appeared to him, that snowy night in this same field. Could his famous Truth be merely the stuff of dreams?

Ticker opened his mouth to let out the long strident call of the elderly cock pheasant, that sound which has echoed in our woods from time immemorial. A cry of despair? Or a clarion call to every one of us? And his Test began.

One of the Men saw him, and raised His hand to point. The Man beside Him turned. Now all eyes were upon Ticker. But no Man moved. No Man raised His gun. And Ticker Khan strode on.

He has described to us how still everything seemed. Only he, in the entire landscape, was moving. Slowly, with measured tread, head held high and tail well clear of the mud, he advanced toward the waiting Men. He had assumed he was in for a most alarming experience. Now he found himself wondering, hoping against hope, whether the sheer act of striding forth might not be all that Man required.

But the Test, when it came, was worse than anything he had anticipated. The first movement was from a Man who ran forward two paces and then picked up a large stone, about the size of a well-filled crop. This he flung, with very great force, toward Ticker. If it had hit him it would certainly have killed him, but this would have been contrary to Man's plan. It fell, as intended, to the side of him and covered the whole of one wing with a horrible cloying mud. Ticker Khan marched on, and already there were shouts of approval from the Men in the line.

The next trial was infinitely worse. A huge yellow dog bounded across the field. It came at Ticker from one side, while he pretended not to notice it, and then—baring its fangs, framed by those sinister black lips and gums—it picked him up. In one continuous movement, hardly pausing in its stride, it spread wide its jaws and swept Ticker Khan off his feet. Even now he maintained his composure. The apostles (those few who witnessed the walk and survived) have told us that although his two legs were now sticking straight up in the air, they continued to go through the motions of walking in exactly the same rhythm as before he was disturbed.

The dog deposited Ticker at the feet of one of the Men, whereupon Ticker stood up, rearranged his feathers, raised his head and tail, and marched on. And then perhaps the most extraordinary thing of all happened—certainly it was the one which surprised Ticker most at the time. He had barely got back into his stride when the Man took three quick paces and kicked him.

It was not a gentle kick. It was a heavy blow,

from the full swing of a powerful leg and a solid leather boot. Ticker rejoices in it now, but at the time it almost knocked him unconscious. It lifted him into the air, and this—as he later came to appreciate—was Man's hidden purpose. For at this moment, says Ticker, he experienced more strongly than ever before the urge to fly. There he was, up in the air, with the Man and the dog below, and a sudden beat of his wings could carry him to safety. For all our sakes he had the strength to resist. He fell on his side, on that same bruised wing which was spattered with mud. Again, more slowly, he righted himself and walked on.

And now finally the Man in the Great House, the Man Himself, came forward. All the apostles agree that He was coming to offer Ticker Khan the final accolade—to congratulate him on having resisted that last and most insidious temptation to fly—for He not only raised His hat to Ticker, He actually threw it toward him. And then He started calling to him, and running toward him with arms outstretched. To do what? To embrace him? To clasp him to His breast?

Alas, we do not yet know. For at that very moment there was a cry of OVA from one of the beaters, that terrible cry so familiar from every Ordeal. It means, as we have long known, that somebody is flying toward the guns. And indeed there now appeared old Faker Khan, an incredibly decrepit bird, blind in one eye and deaf in both ears, laboriously making his way over the tops of the trees. He must have been the only pheasant in all the woods not to have heard of Ticker's walk. Surprised by a dog or a beater's stick, he was lumbering his way out as though this were an ordinary

Ordeal and today but a day of the week.

It is because of Faker Khan that we do not yet know what precise form Man's final acceptance of Ticker was about to take. The cry of OVA distracted all the Men's attention. One of Them raised His gun, and Faker fell. The shot caused panic in the woods, among all those pheasants who but for this might immediately have followed Ticker's example and walked out to their glory. Instead they now flew, low and clumsily, out from the woods. There was unprecedented carnage. Even Dreer Khan, whose curiosity had finally overcome his disapproval, was among them. He can hardly have been ten feet off the ground when he was hit. He lurched on for a few yards with only his legs broken before being riddled with a second blast, which carried away a bunch of his softer feathers to hang in the air long after him. If his religious beliefs had any truth in them, I fear he would have stood no chance at all of becoming a Blessed Morsel. It was one of the side walls and down the drive for him.

Ticker Khan stood for a while near the Man in the Great House, in case he wished to continue whatever ceremony had been interrupted. But the moment had passed, and with so much else going on the Man seemed to show no further interest in Ticker. So he walked on, increasingly aware now of his wounds from the boot and the dog's teeth, until he reached the shelter of the line of firs. He

rested there till nightfall, before returning to begin his mission.

☸

I too, at much the same time, was coming back that night from my own less glorious day. With the frivolous chatter of partridges still in my ear, I was picking a stealthy way back into the copse when I became aware of a great crowd under the forked beech tree. I edged myself toward the front. There stood Ticker Khan. There was congealed blood on his wing, where the toe of the boot had struck him, and the wing itself trailed, apparently broken. But in his eye there was the light of indescribable joy and it was this—when combined with the sight of his broken wing—which held the onlookers spellbound. For what pheasant had ever before rejoiced with a broken wing?

"What need have I of a wing?" he asked. "I have walked with Man. Who ever saw a Man fly?"

"He has walked with Man. He has walked with Man." The word buzzed round. The Pheasant Who Walked with Man—already that night they gave him his well-known title. And the apostles moved among the crowd telling details of what they had seen.

But I stood, my ears still filthy with the sound of partridges. And then my own personal miracle occurred. For suddenly Ticker Khan's eye, that glowing eye, fell upon me.

"Have you heard the Truth?" he asked. "Have you heard it, Bamber Khan?"

"Yes." I bowed my head.

"Then you shall write it." For I was the first writer that his eye had fallen upon that holy evening, on the day that he walked with Man.

And thus it was that I became his Personal Secretary. And thus it was that my own night turned into day. And thus it was that I have taken my part in the tireless mission of these summer months, helping to bring the word to every pheasant before the next Ordeal, which shall be the Last Ordeal, the Day of Jubilation when pheasants everywhere shall become one with Man, and among them my own humble and sinful self, and among them you too, my elegant reader, unless you choose to live without the Truth in an eternal round of Fear and Ordeals and Death. And thus it is that I am entrusted with the task, by Ticker Khan himself, of bringing to you in this little book the irrefutable evidence of that Truth.

There are three Holy Days. Two have passed, and the third is to come. They are:

THE DAY OF REVELATION

*when Pecker Khan appeared
to Ticker Khan and the
Truth was seen.*

THE DAY OF CONFIRMATION

*when Ticker Khan walked with
Man and the Truth was shown.*

THE DAY OF JUBILATION

*when we shall all walk with
Man and the Truth shall be known.*

Unceasingly the mission has gone forward and by now there can be no pheasant on the Estate whom the Word has not reached. It was carried in the spring to young couples gathering bracken for the nest, and in the summer they in turn passed it on to their fledgling young; it was brought to this year's foster-fowl while they were still in their pens, in spite of furious interruptions from the reactionary old chickens who have charge of them; it has been discussed, these long light evenings, in countless study groups up in the branches. If there is still a pheasant who has not heard the glad tidings he can only be, like poor old Faker Khan, stone deaf.

Meanwhile the specialists among us have been concerned with other tasks, and modesty need not prevent my mentioning here my own share in one of the most important of these—the establishing of the sacred text. Except for the one word OVA, which we had heard so often, we had never before made any attempt to write down the sayings of Man. But what was said to Ticker Khan during his Test did seem of such prime importance that a very great effort was made to record it. Not surprisingly, Ticker himself had only the vaguest impressions of the exact sounds that the Men were making at the time, but exhaustive statements were taken from every one of the spectators who survived. After allowing for wild variations in spelling, the results had from the start a most encouraging consistency. A team of scholars led by myself collated the different versions, and translated them into a uniform spelling which seemed best to convey the sounds toward which our informants were groping. Ticker Khan readily accepted our result as the authorized version, and the phrases, though still not fully understood, have now long been familiar to every pheasant as the sacred text of our Faith, commonly referred to as the Ten Words of Man.

LUKATHAT

GEDDUP GEDDUP

GODAWMITEY LUKATHAT

CRISEYESS LUKATHAT

WOTAYELLABUGGA LUKATHAT

CRISESAKE

It is not yet known precisely what was meant by Man when He spoke these words to Ticker Khan, but my scholars and I have spent many long hours on the intepretation of the sacred text and we are making progress. All we can say for certain at this stage is that the word LUKATHAT, which will be seen to appear no less than four times, means Salvation. LUKATHAT is the condition to which all pheasants must aspire. LUKATHAT is the reward of those who have the courage not to fly. LUKATHAT is the blessed peace which shall come to those who walk with Man.

Our leader Ticker Khan, the Great Pheasant, has made it possible for all of us to achieve LUKA-THAT together this coming autumn. Already the leaves are turning, and there is the beginning of a new carpet in the beech wood. One day soon the Keeper will place the sticks out across the field, and then the Last Ordeal will be upon us, the Final Test, the Day of Jubilation.

Most of us are ready, and the order of the day has been drawn up—the order in which we pheasants shall march, in serried ranks, into the arms of Man.

In front will be Ticker Khan himself, the Pheasant Who Has Already Walked with Man and who now generously offers himself up, for all our sakes, to a second test.

Behind him will march the apostles and others who have done most to spread the Word.

After them will come the ranks of natural-born birds, old cocks first, then young cocks, followed by the young and old hens together.

Finally there will march all the rest—the foster-fowls—arranged in the same order of old cocks, young cocks, hens.

And not far behind the last hen will come myself and two or three members of my staff. From our own point of view this is a most disappointing position on such a day. But alas,

if we are to chronicle this great event, it is essential that we view it with a reasonably broad perspective.

And what of Man?

Does He yet know that His dearest wishes are at last about to be fulfilled? Or does He imagine that the next Ordeal will be as disappointing as any other, with pheasants flying all over the place and falling in our hundreds to His guns?

All we can foretell is the joy that He will experience on that Great Morn, when He and the other Men have lined up across the field and suddenly Ticker Khan steps forth—no longer alone but with rank upon rank of upright pheasants now walking behind him, slow and stately, step by solemn step, toward the waiting guns. And Man shall hear His own Words blazoned forth. For Ticker shall cry LUKATHAT and we his followers shall echo LUKA-THAT and Ticker shall continue to give us courage with that one resounding cry while we repeat behind him the Ten Words of Man.

> *Ticker Khan*   LUKATHAT
> *The serried ranks*   LUKATHAT
> *Ticker Khan*   LUKATHAT
> *The serried ranks*   GEDDUP GEDDUP

Ticker Khan	LUKATHAT
The serried ranks	GODAWMITEY LUKATHAT
Ticker Khan	LUKATHAT
The serried ranks	CRISEYESS LUKATHAT
Ticker Khan	LUKATHAT
The serried ranks	WOTAYELLABUGGA LUKATHAT
Ticker Khan	LUKATHAT
The serried ranks	CRISESAKE
Ticker Khan	LUKATHAT
The serried ranks	LUKATHAT!

And it shall be LUKATHAT. Whatever buffets Man may have in store for us on that day, it shall be LUKATHAT. However He may beat us, set His dogs upon us, cast us in the mud, it shall be LUKATHAT. And Man shall finally open His arms and take us into His House.

And then? Afterwards? What, when we have attained it, is LUKATHAT?

As yet, we cannot tell. Each of us has his own ideas of what may lie beyond. Images of well-watered glades, scattered raisins, or fields of ripe corn swaying eternally in the breeze, these are but the feeble approximations of poetry. Perhaps there may be more truth in metaphor, in the idea that where we now tremble even to approach Man, we shall walk side by side with Him; where we now eat alone in His fields and woods, we shall henceforth share His meal; where we have in the past died for Him, we shall in future live for Him.

What we do know for certain, through Faith and through the brave example of Ticker Khan, is that it will be a more blessed existence, because closer, through all eternity, to Mankind.

And the Kingdom of

LUKATHAT

shall be ours!